STAG

'Oh, ⟨ ⟩ouliet! If only I could ... er ...' James
traile⟨ ⟩ off. This time he had *definitely* seen it.
A ho⟨ ⟩ble-looking man in armour, carrying his
own ⟨ ⟩d under his arm, was flickering in and
out o⟨ ⟩ght a few paces behind Gordon Carver.

'Ja⟨ ⟩s! Your lines!' bellowed Mr Thomas.

'B⟨ ⟩ sir!' James cried. 'Can't you see ...'

'N⟨ ⟩ now, James!' shouted the drama teacher.
'Ale⟨ ⟩nder – can we have some lights, please?'

A⟨ ⟩ne back of the room, Alexander flicked the
spotl⟨ ⟩ht switch on and aimed it at James.
Notl⟨ ⟩ng. He checked the plug.

'S⟨ ⟩ry, sir!' he shouted. 'It was working earlier!'

He unscrewed the back of the light and peered
inside.

'Eugh! What the ...' he cried, reeling back and
covering his nose. The lighting rig wobbled, and
a shower of small, wriggly maggots rained down.

12209222

St Sebastian's School in Grimesford is the pits. No, really – it is.

Every year, the high school sinks a bit further into the boggy plague pit beneath it and, every year, the ghosts of the plague victims buried underneath it become a bit more cranky.

Egged on by their spooky ringleader, Edith Codd, they decide to get their own back – and they're willing to play dirty. *Really* dirty.

They kick up a stink by causing as much mischief as inhumanly possible so as to get St Sebastian's closed down once and for all.

But what they haven't reckoned on is year-seven new boy, James Simpson and his friends Alexander and Lenny.

The question is, are the gang up to the challenge of laying St Sebastian's paranormal problem to rest, or will their school remain forever frightful?

There's only one way to find out . . .

www.too-ghoul.com

TOO GHOUL FOR SCHOOL

STAGE FRIGHT

B. STRANGE

EGMONT

Special thanks to:

Matt Crossick, St John's Walworth Church of England Primary School and Belmont Primary School

SANDWELL LIBRARY & INFORMATION SERVICE	
12209222	
Bertrams	24/06/2008
CFSCH	£4.99
BH	

Stage Fright first published in Great Britain 2008
by Egmont UK Limited
239 Kensington High Street, London W8 6SA

Text & illustrations © 2008 Egmont UK Ltd
Text by Matt Crossick
Illustrations by Pulsar Studios

ISBN 978 1 4052 3929 5

1 3 5 7 9 10 8 6 4 2

A CIP catalogue record for this title is available
from the British Library

Typeset by Avon DataSet Ltd, Bidford on Avon, Warwickshire
Printed and bound in Great Britain by the CPI Group

All rights reserved. No part of this publication may be reproduced,
stored in a retrieval system, or transmitted, in any form or by
any means, electronic, mechanical, photocopying, recording
or otherwise, without the prior permission of the publisher.

'I really like how the main characters
are explained'

Sam, age 8

'My favourite character is James because
I like his good looks'

Nathan, age 7

'I think this series is AWESOME!'

Hoia, age 8

'Totally gross and spooky because you never
know what will happen next'

Alex, age 9

'I think that *Too Ghoul for School* books are
GREAT because of the supernatural events'

Jack, age 8

**We want to hear what *you* think about
Too Ghoul for School! Visit:**

www.too-ghoul.com

**for loads of cool stuff to do
and a whole lotta grot!**

School versus...

James Simpson

Has to 'brace' himself to wear tights in front of the whole school!

Lighting techinician and skeleton smasher!

Alexander Tick

This boy's got a bone to pick with those plague-pit ghosts...

Lenny Maxwell

...Ghoul!

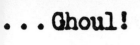

ould it be curtains for this spooky old hag?

Edith Codd

This plucky little ghost is a real show-stopper

William Scroggins

Prefers scoffing leeches to treading the boards

Ambrose Harbottle

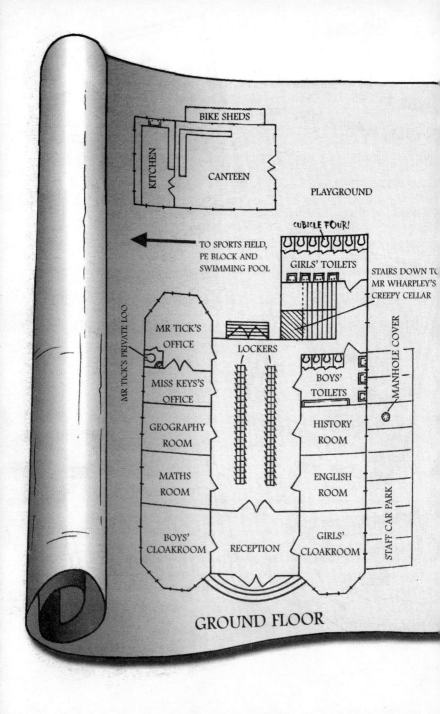

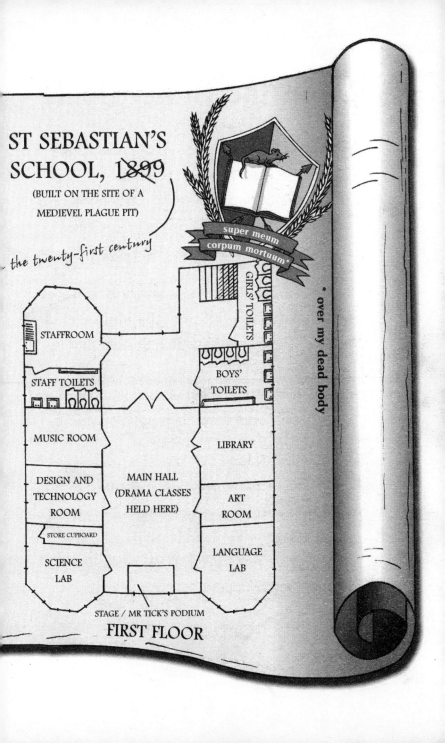

About the Black Death

The Black Death was a terrible plague that is believed to have been spread by fleas on rats. It swept through Europe in the fourteenth century, arriving in England in 1348, where it killed over one third of the population.

One of the Black Death's main symptoms was **foul-smelling boils all over the body called 'buboes'.** The plague was so infectious that its victims and their families were locked in their houses until they died. Many villages were abandoned as the disease wiped out their populations.

So many people died that graveyards overflowed and bodies lay in the street, so special **'plague pits'** were dug to bury the bodies. Almost every town and village in England has a plague pit somewhere underneath it, so watch out when you're digging in the garden . . .

Dear Reader

As you may have already guessed, B. Strange is not a real name.

The author of this series is an ex-teacher who is currently employed by a little-known body called the Organisation For Spook Termination (Excluding Demons), or O.F.S.T.(E.D.). 'B. Strange' is the pen name chosen to protect his identity.

Together, we felt it was our duty to publish these books, in an attempt to save innocent lives. The stories are based on the author's experiences as an O.F.S.T.(E.D.) inspector in various schools over the past two decades.

Please read them carefully - you may regret it if you don't . . .

Yours sincerely
The Publisher.

PS - Should you wish to file a report on any suspicious supernatural occurrences at your school, visit **www.too-ghoul.com** and fill out the relevant form. We'll pass it on to O.F.S.T.(E.D.) for you.

PPS - All characters' names have been changed to protect the identity of the individuals. Any similarity to actual persons, living or undead, is purely coincidental.

CONTENTS

CHAPTER 1
ROMEO AND GHOULIET

'Out the way! Coming through!'

James Simpson dropped his school bag and barged his way to the front of the crowd. Lenny Maxwell was already there, staring at a poster stuck to the St Sebastian's school noticeboard.

'What's going on?' James asked his friend. 'They're not holding another custard-eating contest are they? I spent three days in the toilet after the last one!'

Lenny shook his head. 'Nah. Nothing as exciting as that,' he grunted. 'They're putting on a school play. I don't fancy it much myself – sounds too much like hard work!'

James studied the poster. It was fixed to the noticeboard with a bit of old chewing gum. 'WANTED!' it said in big letters. 'ACTORS TO STAR IN ROMEO AND GHOULIET! SIGN UP HERE!'

'Yeah. Sounds duller than one of Mr Tick's assemblies,' James agreed.

'And what's worse, we'd have to miss science lessons to go to rehearsals!' said a voice behind them.

Alexander Tick squeezed through the chattering crowd and peered at his best friends over a huge pile of textbooks.

'Did you say we get to miss science lessons, Alexander?' Lenny asked, raising his eyebrows.

'Yes – terrible, isn't it?' Alexander replied. 'Imagine – what kind of idiot would want to do a stupid school play instead of learning about the magic of science with Mr Watts? Why, you'd have to be some kind of . . . James! What are you doing?'

James had grabbed a pen from Alexander's blazer pocket and was frantically scribbling his name on the sign-up sheet.

'Missing science?' he cried. 'Count me in!'

Lenny snatched the pen off him and added his name to the list.

'Too right, mate!' he nodded. 'I'd sign up to be a ballet dancer if it meant getting out of Mr Watt's weekly boring-o-thon!'

Alexander scowled at them both.

'All I can say is Mr Watts has more talent in his little finger than any of those rubbish footballers you like so much!'

Lenny rolled his eyes. 'I know the headmaster's son is *meant* to be a nerd, Stick,' he groaned, 'but you really take your duties too far!'

James peered at the small print on the poster. 'Yeah – and they need a lighting engineer for the play, too. Why don't you sign up?'

'Lighting engineer?' said Alexander, his ears pricking up. 'I suppose that would be a rather interesting project! I could investigate the effect of rewiring the stage lights with improved resistors. But what about Mr Watts?'

4

James grabbed the pen and wrote Alexander's name on the list.

'Oh, come on, Stick!' he laughed. 'You spend every weekend reading about science. You spend every lunchtime boring us about it. And Lenny and I are still mentally scarred from the science-themed birthday party you made us go to. So missing a few lessons won't do you any harm!'

'Hey – the effects of that chemical wore off after a week,' said Alexander. 'Anyway, I've got to go. The Gorilla is making me do his maths homework for him!'

'Shhhh!' hissed James with a frown.

'What?' cried Alexander. 'That big oaf is too stupid to do it himself, so he bullies year seven kids like me into it. I'm going to put the wrong answers down, anyway!'

Lenny kicked Alexander in the shin. 'Shut up, you idiot!'

'Oh, don't tell me you're scared!' Alexander

continued. 'That meat-head will never find out. He might be a brute, but he's got a brain the size of a p-p-p . . .'

Alexander tailed off. James and Lenny were staring over his shoulder.

'H-h-he's behind me, isn't he?' Alexander whimpered. A fierce punch to the back of the head confirmed his theory.

'Owwwww!'

'If I didn't need my maths homework by lunchtime, I'd squash you for that!' Gordon 'The Gorilla' Carver grunted. 'Now do it!'

Alexander scurried off while the big year eight wrinkled up his nose and peered at the noticeboard.

'Right!' he boomed. 'What about this play?'

James looked surprised. 'I didn't have you down as an actor, Gordon!' he said nervously.

The bully scowled at him and snatched the pen from his hand.

'Shut it, squirt!' he muttered. 'Anything to get out of lessons! And I hear there's fighting in it. *Proper* fighting!'

He thumped his huge fist against the noticeboard, which wobbled off its rickety frame and came crashing down on to Lenny's toe.

'This school is the pits!' James grumbled.

'Tell me about it!' Lenny agreed. 'If it doesn't get sorted out soon, they'll have to add hard hats to the uniform!'

'Hello, Mr Tick speaking. How can I help?'

The headmaster yawned down the phone and stroked his 'Best Headmaster in the World' mug.

'Uh-huh. You're an ex-pupil. How interesting.'

He yawned again and picked up his computer mouse, absent-mindedly moving playing cards about on the screen. He hated phone calls – they disturbed his solitaire practice.

'Well, we don't normally allow visits to the school from ex-pupils, I'm afraid . . .' he said grumpily. 'Now, if there's nothing else . . .'

But he froze halfway through hanging up.

'What? A donation to the school? *How* much?' he cried. 'W-w-well maybe I was a bit hasty. Of *course* you can visit the school, Lord Goldsworthy. Why not come down and see our school play? And we can talk some more about this donation!'

He was still punching the air when Miss Keys, the school secretary, burst into his office.

'Mr Tick! It's the PE block!' she cried hysterically. 'The roof has blown clean off!'

Mr Tick frowned. 'Well? Does it really *need* a roof?' he grumbled, eyeing his computer screen.

'But the children are getting drenched in the rain!' the secretary wailed. 'One of the classrooms is filling with water!'

Mr Tick glanced out of the window at the PE

block. The roof was over in the playing field. Some frightened, damp faces were pressed up against one of the mucky windows.

'Then send them over some arm-bands from the swimming pool!' tutted the headmaster. 'This school isn't made of money, you know!'

As Miss Keys shuffled meekly out, he grabbed a pencil and a piece of paper.

'PLANS FOR LORD GOLDSWORTHY'S MONEY' he wrote in big letters.

'No. 1: NEW HEADMASTER'S OFFICE'.

He sat back and admired his list. 'Yes. That's what this school needs!' he smiled. 'A new building – for the best headmaster in the world!'

Mr Tick's voice echoed around his office, down the pipes in the corner, and into the dark, slimy pit deep under the school. In a corner of this pit, pressing her ear to the rusty pipe, was a disgusting old hag with flaky, rotting skin, fuzzy hair and bony witch's fingers. She let out a rasping groan.

'A new building?' the hag screeched. 'That'll mean even more noise from that pesky school!'

She put her pasty, peeling ear to the pipe again.

'I'll show them, though!' she cackled. 'No one messes with Edith Codd!'

CHAPTER 2
BRACE YOURSELF

'Hang on a sec. I'm a *skeleton*?' cried Lenny, picking up a black costume. 'How come I have to prance around dressed as a skeleton, and you get to play the lead role?' he moaned at James.

'Maybe it's because you're lankier than the *real* skeleton in the biology lab!' James joked. Lenny wasn't amused.

'I'm not lanky!' he moaned. 'I'm just tall for my age!'

All around the room, pupils were struggling into Roman outfits or dreadful skeleton costumes.

Lenny squeezed into his, his long legs poking out of the bottoms by a mile.

'Not lanky, eh, Lenny?' laughed James, as his friend tried to make his top and his trousers meet.

'This costume is rubbish!' Lenny moaned in response. 'It's just a pair of black pyjamas with white tape stuck on it for the bones!'

'Why don't you just not eat until the night of the play, and go on stage naked?' said James, who was struggling to wrap a pair of bright pink braces over his shoulders.

Lenny grabbed one of them and pinged James hard in the face.

'Owww! That hurts!' cried James. He tried to wrestle the braces back on, but they both pinged upwards at once, smacking his cheeks hard, and causing his trousers to fall down just as several year-eight girls swanned into the hall – the blonde Stacey Carmichael in the lead. James blushed furiously as she started giggling uncontrollably.

Mr Thomas followed the girls in. 'So!' the drama teacher cried, looking at the assembled cast. 'You want to be actors! You want to tread the boards! You want to hear the roar of the crowd!'

'Actually, we just wanted to miss science!' grumbled James, pulling his trousers up.

'Well, you're in for a treat, I can tell you!' Mr Thomas continued. 'I wrote the play myself – and, as you all know, I was very nearly a big Hollywood scriptwriter!'

Lenny groaned. 'In other words – the school was too stingy to fork out for twenty-five copies of an *actual play*, so he had to write one!'

'It's a modern-day romance between our two lead characters – Romeo and Ghouliet, played by James and Stacey,' said Mr Thomas, pointing at James, who was still wrestling with his braces. 'They're kept apart by two terrible armies. One skeleton army – led by Lenny Maxwell – and one Roman army brought forward in time, led by Gordon Carver!'

Gordon was already in full Roman armour, waving his sword about and making throat-cutting gestures at Alexander.

'Alexander – you'll do the lights!' said Mr Thomas. 'You'll have to go and get them from Mr Wharpley's cellar!'

But Alexander had his hand up. 'Why a skeleton

14

army, sir?' he asked.

Mr Thomas frowned. 'Well, I've noticed some of you taking a strong interest in the supernatural!' he answered, looking at the three friends.

Alexander carried on. 'And what about the Roman army? Scientifically, there's no way an entire Roman legion could be transported materially through a wormhole in time without a serious temporal shift occurring!'

Lenny groaned. 'Will I ever be able to escape from science?' he muttered.

'Not if you hang around with Stick, you won't!' laughed James.

Mr Thomas thought for a moment. 'Er . . . you can't apply *logic* to *art*, Alexander!' he said. 'Now let's get on with the play, shall we?'

'In other words,' Lenny smirked, 'the school had a job lot of Roman costumes left over from last year's play!'

'Ready, everybody?' cried Mr Thomas, clapping his hands. 'Scene one – *action!*'

As Alexander sloped off to find Mr Wharpley, the school caretaker, the pyjama-clad skeletons shuffled across the stage towards the Romans, tripping over the tape dangling off their costumes. The Romans tried to march towards them, but their cardboard visors kept blocking their eyes.

'Oaargh!'

Two Roman soldiers fell off the stage in a pile.

As Alexander dragged a big light into the hall, Gordon grabbed his sword and leapt to the front of the stage, waving at him and making bloodthirsty roaring noises.

'Good acting, Gordon!' praised Mr Thomas. 'Very fierce!'

Alexander gulped and backed away from the stage. 'Er. . . I don't think he's acting, sir!' he whimpered, grabbing a soldering iron for protection.

'OOOOOF!'

Two skeletons slipped over their trailing pyjama legs and went flying into some Romans, who were stumbling blindly round the stage.

Just as James was thinking that even two hours of science was better than this rubbish, the hall door opened with a loud *smash* and Mr Tick strode into the room.

'Aha! My budding actors!' he beamed, jumping

on to the stage. 'I've got brilliant news! The famous Lord Goldsworthy – who, as you all know, was a pupil here in the nineteen-sixties – is coming to visit. And he wants to see your play!'

Everyone looked at him blankly.

'Lord Goldsworthy has very kindly agreed to donate a *large sum of money* to the school!' Mr Tick continued, pacing up and down. 'Money that the school badly needs to build a new headmaster's office!' he bellowed, stamping his foot. The stage wobbled and some plaster fell off the crumbling ceiling on to a Roman soldier's head.

James put his hand up. 'Couldn't we spend some of the money on repairing the school, sir?' he asked, looking nervously at the sagging ceiling. Mr Tick frowned and straightened his tie.

'Repairing the school?' he said. 'Why, we haven't got the funds to go about fixing every little thing that breaks round here! Do you know how much it would cost to . . .'

He was about to continue when a delivery man in red overalls wandered into the school hall, carrying a large box.

'I've got a brand-new Solitaire-O-Rama games computer here for a Mr Tick!' he said, dropping the box on the floor. 'Where do you want it?'

Mr Tick looked awkwardly at the pupils in front of him. 'Er . . . just leave it in my office, thanks!' he hissed, shooting the delivery man an evil look.

'The point is,' he boomed, 'Lord Goldsworthy is going to visit, so this play had better be good! Or else there will be *big trouble*! Now off you all go, rehearsal is over.'

The cast cheered, except for Lenny, who wasn't paying attention. He was crawling about on all fours. Mr Thomas scowled at Mr Tick as he strode out of the hall.

'What about my rehearsal?' he mumbled at the retreating headmaster, but Mr Tick was gone – followed closely by the rest of Mr Thomas's cast.

'Has anyone seen my skeleton mask?' said
Lenny as the last few actors sprinted from the hall.

'Oh, shut up, Lenny!' said James, flicking through
his script. His face was rather pink.

'Shut up yourself, fat . . . why are you blushing?'
asked Lenny, climbing to his feet.

'Cos I've just read the last scene, you idiot!' cried
James. 'And I have to *kiss* Stacey in it!'

Lenny cracked up. '*Yuck*!' he guffawed, dancing
round James making big kissing noises. 'James and
Stacey, sitting in a tree, K.I.S.– *Oooooof*!'

James stuck a foot out and sent Lenny
sprawling.

'Yeah, well, at least I'm not wearing pyjamas on
stage!' he grumbled.

CHAPTER 3
THE BORED ROOM

William Scroggins was bored. Bored, bored, *bored*.
He'd been haunting the dingy, smelly plague pit
he had been buried in for over six hundred and
fifty years, and it was *boring*. He splashed through
a puddle of sewage and headed for the big
amphitheatre in the middle of the pit.

If only there were more young ghosts in here! he
thought. *I wish I had some friends my own age!*

William slouched through a slimy hole and into
the big, smelly room. It was filled with ghosts of all
shapes and sizes – rotting, stinking ghosts with

21

waxy faces and peeling skin.

'Bor-ing, bor-ing, bor-ing!' he muttered, pushing through the crowd, until he tripped over a severed head and went sprawling on the floor.

'Owww!' he yelped.

'Gotchya!' cried the head. 'Good one, eh, Ambrose?' it chuckled to the ghost next to it.

'Hilarious. That's only the three-thousand-seven-hundred-and-forty-fifth time you've got me!' moaned William.

'Hey – you laughed the first time, matey!' said the Headless Horseman, picking up his head and tucking it under his arm – where it had lived since it was chopped off in 1643.

William sighed. 'The first time was four hundred and thirty years ago!' he scowled. 'Anyway, I'm *bored*!'

Ambrose Harbottle yawned next to him and casually poked a large, wriggly leech that was crawling across his hand. He had been a leech farmer when he was alive, and had never lost his love of the slimy creatures.

'Well, prepare to get even more bored!' he said. 'Edith's about to give one of her rants!'

William groaned. That's all he needed . . . the tedious old hag ranting at him for an hour. Suddenly, a disgusting sharp voice screeched round the room.

'Right, you horrible lot! Get ready to listen!'

Edith Codd clambered on to a barrel at the front of the room, a bit of rotting flesh dropping off her leg with a 'splat'. She smoothed down her matted, frizzy hair and took a deep breath.

'Here we go!' sighed Ambrose.

'It's time we got rid of that pesky school once and for all!' screeched Edith, her voice sounding like fingernails on a blackboard. 'It's making this plague pit a total misery!'

'Well, *that* and the fact it's full of *dead people!*' grumbled Ambrose.

'The noisy pupils' feet! Their leaky sewage pipes! The constant din! This was a *respectable, quiet* plague pit until that school was built!' she carried on.

'It was quiet until Edith was chucked in it, that's for sure!' muttered Bertram Ruttle, a cheeky, thin ghost at the back of the room.

'And now, I've got news that's going to shock you all. *Horrify you*. Send you into fits of rage!' Edith squawked, working herself up into a frenzy.

'They're planning on building a *new block!*' she bellowed. 'A *new building*! What do you think of that then, eh?'

Edith stood staring at the ghosts with her hands on her hips.

The room was silent.

'Can we go now?' asked Bertram from the back.

'*No, you may not!*' roared Edith, pulling out a clump of hair and hurling it at him. 'You lot are a *disgrace* to ghostkind! That school is about to get

even worse, and you're just sitting there picking your noses!'

The Headless Horseman looked up guiltily. 'Sorry!' he said. 'Does anyone else want some?'

Edith started to scowl and shake violently. Little bits of foam were fizzing out of her mouth, splattering the ghosts in the front row.

'You lot are *useless!*' the old hag screamed, kicking an unfortunate skeleton in the ribs. He collapsed with a tinkling, bony noise.

'Well, what do you want us to do about it?' cried Bertram.

'*Aha!*' cried Edith, slapping her putrid, bony thigh. 'At last! Some interest! Well, I have a plan!'

She turned to the muddy wall behind her, and started scratching at it with an old finger bone.

'You started this!' hissed Ambrose to Bertram. 'She'll never stop now!'

But Edith wasn't listening. She was drawing a diagram on the wall.

'The school is holding a play!' she cried, scribbling furiously. 'It will take place *here*, in the school hall. The Lord with the money will be arriving *here*, before watching the play. All we have to do is raise a skeleton army from the dead, totally ruin the play, horrify the Lord, and the new block is history.'

She dropped her finger bone and turned expectantly to see the ghosts' reaction.

The room was empty.

In a slimy corridor deep inside the plague pit, Ambrose watched the Headless Horseman fiddle with the enormous, bloody sword he carried with him everywhere.

'Any . . . minute . . . *now*!' he said.

'Grooooaaaaargh!'

Edith's furious scream echoed round the plague

pit, rattling bones and blowing slime off the walls.

'I'll show you all! I don't need your help!' the echo wailed. Ambrose sniggered.

'Fancy a leech, anyone?' he smiled, offering a box of the wriggling, slug-like creatures round the room.

'No thanks, Ambrose!' said William, squeezing himself up a dripping sewage pipe in the corner. 'I'm off to see this play!'

Ambrose nodded. 'Be good!' he warned. 'And remember to stay invisible!'

At the other end of the sewage pipe, William slithered up the U-bend and splashed out of a filthy lavatory in the boys' toilets.

'Eugh!' he muttered, shaking some sewage off.

William peered over the top of the cubicle and snuck out. As he went, he caught a glimpse of his reflection in the mirror. He was short, skinny, and his ghostly skin was stretched tight over his skull. In fact, he looked almost exactly like Alexander Tick – only *deader*.

He concentrated hard, made himself invisible, and slipped into the school hall, hardly able to contain his excitement. When he was alive, William's mother had taken him to see a touring play on the village green every year. He loved the theatre!

What he saw, however, made his jaw drop. And a rotten tooth fall out. Boys in black pyjamas were stumbling round the stage, bumping into other boys in silly helmets.

'No! *No!*' cried a teacher from the front. 'I said *skeletons attack*! You lot are *useless*!'

As the boys in silly helmets fell over in a heap, William recognised James Simpson striding on to the stage.

'Your eyes are so blue, I could *owwwww*!' he

screamed as one of his braces pinged up again and
caught him in the eye. He stumbled over a boy in
pyjamas, grabbed on to the curtain for support,
and brought the whole thing tumbling down on to
the stage, covering everybody on it.

'Who turned out the lights?'

'This isn't in my script!'

'What's going on?'

William watched James's friend Lenny Maxwell

laugh so hard that his tight trousers split, and he had to shuffle off the stage covering his behind with a wooden shield.

William sighed and headed back to the toilets. Plays were better in his day, he decided. *Much* better.

CHAPTER 4
COSTUME DRAMA

'How do bees get to school?' asked Alexander, bounding up to his two friends.

Lenny groaned. 'I've no idea, Stick.'

'On the school *buzz*!' Alexander guffawed, bending over with laughter.

James rolled his eyes in despair.

'What do you call a boy with the world's un-funniest joke collection?' he asked.

'Erm . . . Alexander Tick?' guessed Lenny.

'Correct!' James smirked. 'And now . . . another hour of The Worst Play in the World!'

'Just think of the science we're missing, James,' said Lenny.

'True!' James sighed. 'But this play *is* horrendous. Have you heard the cheesy lines I have to spout?'

'You've got it easy!' Lenny snorted. 'I have to prance about in my two-sizes-too-small pyjamas looking like a ... like a ...'

'Like a total freak?' piped up Alexander.

'Cheers, Stick!' frowned Lenny.

'Hey – at least you two aren't in mortal danger!' said Alexander. 'I electrocuted myself *three times* yesterday trying to fix those prehistoric stage lights.'

'I just thought you'd got yourself a fashionable haircut at last!' said Lenny, as the three boys walked into the school hall – and stopped dead in their tracks.

'Whoah! Gruesome!' gasped Lenny.

'Urgh! *Sick*!' cried James.

Alexander wiped his glasses.

33

In front of them, sitting on the stage, was a row of the most hideous-looking skeletons they had ever seen. Their white skin was plastered tight over their yellow bones. Their skulls were hollow, with no eyes in the sockets, and they had thick slime encrusted round their rotten teeth.

Alexander approached one and gave it a poke.

'They look rather . . . *real*!' he said.

'Mr Thomas must have ordered some new skeleton costumes!' said James, gasping. 'They look *awesome*!'

Lenny frowned. 'Great. So now I'm the *only one* left in pyjamas?'

He approached a skeleton and nudged its arm. 'Hey – where did you get the new outfit?' he asked. 'Is there one left for me?'

The skeleton wobbled slightly. Some slime oozed out of its ear and dolloped on to Lenny's top.

'I said – is there a costume for me?' he repeated more loudly.

The skeleton opened its mouth, and a maggot crawled round its front teeth and into its nose socket. A low croaking noise came out.

Lenny was about to give the skeleton a good shake when Gordon Carver charged on to the stage, waving a huge metal sword above his head.

'Roaaargh!' he cried, swishing the sword backwards and forwards with both hands. 'Look what I found in the weapons box!'

'E-e-easy there, Gordon!' whimpered Alexander, backing away towards his lighting pile. 'No need to actually try it out!'

'Is that blood dripping off it?' hissed James.

'Probably the remains of his breakfast!' Lenny whispered.

'Well, let's just hope it's ketchup, for Alexander's sake!' said James, as Mr Thomas swept into the room. He was wearing a beret and carrying a copy of *How to Make it in Hollywood* under his arm.

'Are you ready to act, my wonderful cast?' he cried, jumping into a chair. 'Show me scene three! And make sure it's b–b–b–'

He froze, and stared at the skeletons perched on the edge of the stage.

'And wh–wh–who are y–you?' he asked, moving his chair back a few paces. 'W–where are my n–normal skeletons?'

Lenny shuffled on stage in his ridiculous tight

black pyjamas, his stomach poking out from under the top.

'Do I get a new outfit too, sir?' he asked. 'The other skeletons look *really* scary now!'

Mr Thomas eyed the skeletons suspiciously. One of them was pulling his rotten teeth out and flicking them at a frowning Gordon.

'Erm, l–let's not worry about costumes now, Lenny!' the drama teacher said nervously. 'Let's just get on with the scene!'

James stood opposite Stacey Carmichael on the stage and started to read his lines out.

'Oh, Ghouliet!' he wobbled, blushing. 'Your eyes are so beautiful, I could get lost in them!'

Lenny sniggered behind him. One of the skeletons stood up and started to lurch around the stage, poking a bony finger into his eye socket.

'Oh, Romeo, my love!' Stacey cried. 'If only the Romans weren't set against our love! But they'll never let us be together!'

Gordon strode on stage, his big, bloody sword over his shoulder. All the skeletons had now stood up, and were rattling their dry bones as they jolted about. Some were flicking maggots at the cast.

Stacey looked at James quizzically. He shrugged and read on.

'Oh, Ghouliet! Your golden hair glows like the setting sun!'

As Stacey was about to reply, two maggots dropped on to her head and wriggled around her blonde locks. She screamed and flapped frantically at her head, before slipping on some slime, tumbling off the stage and sending Mr Thomas sprawling off his director's chair.

'Oooof!' cried the drama teacher, his beret flying off.

'*What* in the name of *St Sebastian* is going on here?!' bellowed a familiar voice from the back of the hall.

Stacey hastily helped Mr Thomas to his feet as

Mr Tick approached. The headmaster was frowning and carrying a long rolled-up document under his arm.

'Just rehearsing, Mr Tick, sir!' cried Mr Thomas.

Mr Tick strutted forward and inspected the cast. He gave a skeleton a prod.

'Well, I must say, Mr Thomas. These new skeleton costumes do look particularly good. Very scary indeed!'

Mr Thomas was about to reply when Miss Keys burst into the hall.

'Mr Tick! Come quick!' she cried, catching her breath. 'The swimming pool filter has gone crazy! Thirty-eight pupils have been half-drowned in sludge!'

Mr Tick rolled his eyes. 'There's always something with these pesky kids, isn't there?' he complained.

'But we need to do something! At once!' cried Miss Keys.

'Send Mr Wharpley in with a hose!' replied the headmaster sternly. 'We're not having a new filter fitted – we can't afford it!'

As he turned to storm out, he dropped his roll of paper on the floor. Lenny caught a glimpse of it as he scooped it up.

'PLAN FOR LUXURY HEADMASTER'S OFFICE' it said in big letters. 'SOLID GOLD TOILETS PRICE LIST.'

Lenny sighed. 'That's just what this school needs! A luxury loo for the headmaster!'

'Chin up, Lenny!' said James. 'With a bit of luck, he'll flush himself down it!'

At the back of the room, an invisible William was staring, open mouthed, at Stacey Carmichael.

'Her hair! It's so pretty!' he gasped. 'Her teeth! They aren't yellow and rotting! And her skin – it's

not stuck to her skull and peeling off!'

He clutched his hand over where his heart had been before he died.

'Oh, Stacey!' he whispered. 'You're the most beautiful girl I've ever seen!'

As she took to the front of the stage again, he closed his eyes in a dream.

'If only I could be your Romeo!' he sighed.

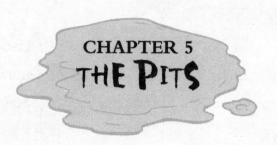

CHAPTER 5
THE PITS

'Where's my sword, you bony rascals?' cried the Headless Horseman, elbowing his way through the noisy throng of skeletons that filled the plague pit. 'I know one of you pests has got it!'

He sent several skulls flying with his elbows before stumbling across Bertram and Ambrose squashed into a corner of the amphitheatre.

'These skeletons are driving me *crazy!*' shouted the horseman over the deafening bone-rattling noise that echoed round the room. 'They're *everywhere!*'

Bertram leant forward.

'You what?' he bellowed over the din. 'You're feeling lazy?'

The horseman shook his head, which was currently tucked under his arm. 'No! I said *crazy*!'

Ambrose crunched on a leech and squeezed over towards him.

'I hear your memory's hazy!' he screamed over the rattling.

'NO! I said *crazy*! *Crazy*! It's these darned skeletons!' the horseman roared.

'I can't hear you!' Ambrose shouted back. 'To be honest, these skeletons are driving me crazy!'

'You're lazy too?' bellowed Bertram. 'What is it with you two?'

'No, *crazy*!' screamed Ambrose. The Headless Horseman groaned.

'Come on!' he shouted, dragging Ambrose and Bertram through the heaving mass. 'We need a place to talk!'

After barging through skeletons for what seemed like an hour, the three ghosts found a small, slimy hole that was still empty, and squeezed themselves in for a break. Ambrose took a juicy-looking leech out of his tin and popped it in his mouth.

'Now, about these skeletons!' said the horseman.

'It's Edith!' moaned Ambrose with his mouth full.

'She heard the headmaster say he *liked* the play, so she just keeps calling up more and more of the things!'

'Ugh! That old hag!' said Bertram, before he felt an icy hand creep round his shoulder.

'And which old hag would that be, Bertram?' said a screeching voice. 'Surely not me?'

The three ghosts turned round to see Edith Codd standing with her hands on her hips, her nostrils flaring with anger.

Bertram let out a low groan.

'I want a word with you lot!' said Edith, prodding each of them in the chest. 'I expect you *all* to help me cause some chaos in that school play today!'

Ambrose finished his leech and licked his fingers.

'Isn't that what all these infernal skeletons are for?' he said, giving one of them an evil look. 'It's not like there's a shortage of the things, is it?'

'Too right!' said Bertram. 'This army of yours is

far more annoying than that school, anyway. I'd rather get rid of *them* than those kids!'

Edith gasped and her eyes glowed a horrid red colour. Some foam dribbled from her flaky nose. She opened her mouth to scream at Bertram.

'W–w–w . . .'

But at the last minute, a change came over her. She shut her mouth, and a mischievous twinkle replaced the angry red look in her eyes.

'So – you want to get rid of the skeletons, do you?' she asked, in a sickly sweet croak.

Bertram and Ambrose nodded.

Edith stroked her chin. A lump of slime dribbled down it and dripped on to her rotting neck.

'Well, they're only here for one reason – to help me spoil that school play,' Edith said. 'And when the play's ruined, I'll be sending them all back to their coffins and muddy graves. So . . .'

'So what?' said Bertram impatiently.

'So the quicker you stupid idiots help me ruin

the play, the quicker this lot will be out of your hair!'

Ambrose ran his hand over his bald scalp. 'What hair?' he asked.

Bertram frowned. 'Can't we just talk about the skeletons?'

Edith's eyes flashed red again.

'I *am* talking about the skeletons, you pathetic excuses for ghosts!' she bellowed at the top of her voice. 'Help me ruin the play, and they'll be gone quicker! Is that simple enough for your useless, six-hundred-year-old brains?'

Ambrose and Bertram looked around at the carnage in the plague pit. Some skeletons were playing jacks with their own knuckle bones on top of Ambrose's leech farm, throwing them in the air and trying to quickly grab them with the rest of their fingers.

'Anything that gets rid of these bony morons is fine by me!' Ambrose grunted.

'Oh, all right!' said Bertram to Edith. 'But they'd better be gone as *soon* as the play is over!'

Edith smiled and rubbed her hands. She gave the Headless Horseman's head – which was now on the floor – a poke with the twisted, black nail on her big toe.

'What?' he grimaced, picking up his head.

'You're helping too!' said the disgusting old hag. 'Now listen up – I've got a plan. But first – where's William? He isn't getting out of this *that* easily . . .'

In the empty school hall, William lunged around the stage, swinging a Roman sword round his head. He had a Roman helmet squeezed over his slimy, mouldy hair and some armour over his stick-thin body.

'I'll save you, Stacey!' he declared, thrusting the sword forwards. 'Have no fear – William's here!'

He twirled across the stage. 'I'm a hero!' he cried. 'And the best actor in the whole wide world!'

He was so busy pretending to be in the play that he didn't notice Miss Keys hurry into the hall. The secretary stopped and stared at the stage.

'Alexander? Is that you?' she said crossly.

William froze. How could she mistake him for

Alexander? Sure, they looked a bit alike. But Alexander didn't have decomposing flesh, putrid white skin and maggoty hair, did he?

'I said, is that you, Alexander?' said Miss Keys. William nodded without opening his mouth.

'Well you'd better get yourself to the school nurse!' said the secretary, going on her way. 'I've never seen you look so pale!'

William heaved a sigh of relief. He'd better stay invisible from now on.

Mr Tick leant over the big architect's plan on his desk. He was drawing on it with a red pencil.

'Now, where should I put the jacuzzi?' he said to himself. 'In front of the tropical fish tank, or next to the window?'

He drew it in next to the fish tank. 'Don't want to see any pesky pupils while I'm in the hot tub!' he smiled to himself.

'And what about the plasma TV? On this wall, or in front of the giant bean bags?'

He was lost in thought when his intercom buzzed.

'Mr Tick, may I have a word?' Miss Keys's voice asked. 'Your son is looking a bit peaky!'

Mr Tick frowned. 'Not now!' he replied into the microphone. 'I'm very busy at the moment!'

He switched off the intercom and put down his pencil.

'All this planning is rather stressful,' he said to himself. 'I think I need to relax over a nice game of solitaire.'

CHAPTER 6
STRESS REHEARSAL

Mr Thomas pushed his new shades down his nose and peered at the cast.

'Hmmm. Yes. Costumes are spot on!' he said, adjusting his beret and sitting back in his director's chair.

'Why is he wearing shades? And that stupid hat?' whispered James.

'I think he's trying to be a Hollywood big-shot!' snorted Lenny, adjusting his skin-tight pyjama bottoms.

'At least he's not letting the fact that he's written

the *worst play ever* get to him,' James replied.

'Now, this is a dress rehearsal, everybody, so I want it to be *perfect*!' Mr Thomas continued. 'It's the big night tonight, and we all know how important this play is to Mr Tick. So let's make it good!'

Unfortunately, everything Mr Thomas said was completely drowned out by the rattling bones of the rowdy skeletons at the back of the stage.

Lenny and James could only make out odd words over the racket.

'Dress . . . big . . . Mr Tick . . . good . . .'

'Did he say Mr Tick looks good in a dress?' asked Lenny.

'Hey, that's my dad you're talking about!' frowned Alexander.

'Shouldn't you be plugging yourself into the mains or something, Stick?' replied Lenny.

'Right!' shouted the drama teacher. 'Let's just get on with it! Scene one – *action*!'

James took to the stage and began reciting his lines. Stacey stood opposite him, looking a bit nervous as a skeleton lurched towards her.

'We begin our story in a land ruled by a terrible skeleton army!' James said loudly. Three of the skeletons started jostling around, bumping into people and rattling their bones.

'Oh! Here comes my fair love! The beautiful Ghouliet!' he carried on, backing away from the skeletons. Stacey followed him across the stage.

'But, oh! Romeo! Here comes the Roman army sent forward in time to kill you! Beware!' she cried, pointing over his shoulder.

Behind James, Gordon Carver strode on, still heaving the massive bloody sword behind him.

'I fear no time-travelling Roman army when I am with you, my love!' said James. But instead of the usual embarrassment he felt at the soppy script, James shuddered – was that a *headless man* he could see following Gordon around the stage?

'Come on, come on!' shouted Mr Thomas. 'This is no time to forget your lines, James!'

James gave himself a slap and carried on. He must be seeing things!

'Oh, Ghouliet! If only I could . . . er . . .' James trailed off. This time he had *definitely* seen it. A horrible-looking man in armour, carrying his own head under his arm, was flickering in and out of sight a few paces behind Gordon Carver.

'James! Your lines!' bellowed Mr Thomas.

'But, sir!' James cried. 'Can't you see . . .'

'Not now, James!' shouted the drama teacher. 'Let's just skip straight to the first song, shall we?'

In the pit, the orchestra started to play. But the usual tuneless din was gone – in its place, an eerie, hollow xylophone sound wafted up, drowning out the song.

'That's bad, even by their standards,' winced Lenny.

'Eurgh! that noise gives me the creeps!' cried James, clamping his hands over his ears.

A deep chill filled the room as the terrible melody sent shudders down everyone's spines.

'Reminds me of the time you tried to learn the violin!' Lenny shivered.

'Er . . . OK, that's quite enough, thanks!' cried Mr Thomas, clapping his hands loudly. 'J–James, carry on! And, Alexander – can we have some lights, please?'

At the back of the room, Alexander flicked the spotlight switch on and aimed it at James. Nothing. He checked the plug.

'Sorry, sir!' he shouted. 'It was working earlier!'

He unscrewed the back of the light and peered inside.

'Eugh! What the . . .' he cried, reeling back and covering his nose.

The inside of the light was filled with stinky black sewage, oozing round the wires and bulb.

'How on earth did that get in there?' Alexander fumed. 'I only fixed it yesterday!'

He stormed over to the stage and gave the lighting rig an angry kick.

'Stupid old gear!'

As the lighting rig wobbled, a shower of small, wriggly maggots rained down from the lights, covering the orchestra completely. They cried out in horror.

'Eeeeeeek!'

'Bleurgh!'

'Gross!'

Within seconds the whole orchestra was in chaos, leaping off their seats and brushing at their clothes and hair. Their disgusted wailing echoed round the hall.

'Get them off me!'

'Help!'

'Yuck!'

The brass players blew hard down their instruments, firing a shower of maggots straight on to the stage. Stacey got a trumpetful right in the face.

'Eeeeeeeek!' she wailed, flailing her arms around and hitting a nearby skeleton. Its skull flew off and rolled along the floor. The drummer started desperately bashing at it with a cymbal.

'What on earth is going on?' cried James, leaping off the stage as another three skeletons crashed into each other in a shower of bones and

slime. A third skeleton swung across the stage on the curtains, knocking the scenery over and sending the rest of the cast diving for cover.

'Children, children, what are you doing? The play, the play!' cried Mr Thomas over the chaos. A skeleton was pouring maggots into his director's chair from a tuba.

'Lenny! Alexander! Over here!' cried James,

pointing to the store cupboard under the stage. 'Take cover!'

The three boys dashed across the room as another piece of scenery clattered to the ground around them, two skeletons dancing on the crumpled wooden heap.

'Good idea!' cried Lenny, skidding across the floor on his knees and into the low, dark cupboard. On his way, he dodged Gordon Carver, who was wrestling a headless man, the two of them grappling for the big metal sword.

'Shut the door! Now!' wailed Alexander as he dived in. James followed him and was about to slam the door shut, when the Headless Horseman's severed head flew out of the chaotic battle scene, rolled along the floor and landed with a 'splat' in Lenny's lap.

'AAAAAAAAAAAARGH!' cried Lenny, flapping at the head. '*Get it off me!*'

James kicked it out of Lenny's lap, and was

about to punt it out of the cupboard with his foot, when the head looked up and smiled at him.

'Enjoying the play?' it said calmly. 'I must say, I thought you were rather good!'

James yelped in surprise, and booted the head with all his might. Lenny slammed the cupboard door shut behind it. He could hear Mr Thomas shouting over the chaos.

'Children! I'd like to run over scene two again! It needs a bit more work!'

Lenny shuddered and kept a tight hold on the door. The boys were quiet for a moment.

'We know what just happened there, don't we?' said James seriously.

'Not again!' said Lenny, shaking his head. 'I thought we got rid of them last time!'

'Of course they're back!' snorted Alexander. 'We're not talking about some noisy neighbours here. We're talking about *ghosts*!'

James nodded. 'And they're angrier than ever!'

CHAPTER 7
THE WORM TURNS

'Ugh! This is *so* unfair!' moaned Lenny. A squelchy knot of maggots oozed round his fingers as he stuffed them into a bin bag.

'Yeah!' cried Alexander, dragging a curtain back towards the stage. 'Why do *we* have to clear up this mess? It wasn't *our* fault!'

James was sweeping up bits of bone with a broom. He stopped for a breather.

'I think Mr Thomas thought it was us mucking stuff up, cos he found us hiding under the stage,' he said.

'Thought it was *us*?' fumed Lenny, shovelling more maggots off the floor. 'Does he think *we* could summon a headless man? Or a troupe of *real* skeletons? Or . . . or . . .'

'Maybe he was wearing his shades?' suggested Alexander. 'Or his beret slipped over his eyes!'

'Maybe he's a total loony!' muttered Lenny, wiping his fingers.

'Anyway, that's not the point!' said James, still leaning on his broom. 'The point is, the ghosts are back, they're haunting this play, and we have to stop them before someone gets hurt!'

Alexander sat on the edge of the stage in silence for a few moments. Then he spoke, rubbing his chin thoughtfully.

'You know, there's a scientific theory that says that ghosts are vulnerable to radioactivity in small doses!' he said, looking at his friends. 'If I could fashion a small reactor using some school computers, concrete from the building site down the road, and some odds and ends from the science cupboard, we could repel the ghosts with a low radioactive beam.'

Lenny and James blinked.

'Translation please, James?' asked Lenny, scratching his head.

'I think he's suggesting we build a ghost gun,' replied James. 'Is that everything you'd need, Stick?'

Alexander carried on rubbing his chin. 'Oh, no – I'd need some plutonium too,' he said.

James groaned.

'Plutonium. Great. Well, thanks for that helpful suggestion.' Lenny snorted. 'I'll just nip down to the corner shop after school and get some, shall I?'

'You could get a ghost trap from the newsagent's next door while you're at it!' laughed James.

'Hey – no need to be sarcastic!' moaned Alexander. 'I'd like to hear *your* great suggestion for getting rid of those ghosts within – oooh – the next *few hours!*'

Lenny thought for a moment. 'We'll have to tell somebody!' he finally said. 'The police! The fire brigade! Someone with a siren on their car.'

'Pffffft!' said Alexander. 'So, we walk down to a fire station. We stroll in, casually inform the firemen that our school play is being haunted, and would they mind coming down and squirting the ghosts with a hose please?'

'Might work?' Lenny shrugged.

'To be fair, Lenny, that *is* one of the worst ideas you've ever had,' said James. 'And I'm including the time you tried to make a go-kart with square wheels.'

'Hey – that had potential!' scowled Lenny, going back to his maggots.

'Well, I think we're just going to have to cancel the play!' said James, finally. 'We can't stop the ghosts, and it's just too dangerous to let everyone in with those skeletons running riot.'

'But how do we cancel it? Mr Thomas will never let us drop out at the last minute!' replied Lenny.

'Yeah – plus my dad is *totally obsessed* with Lord Goldsworthy coming to see it. There's no *way* he'd let us pull out now.'

'What about ghost-proofing?' asked James. 'Any more bright ideas?

Alexander was mopping up bits of knuckle bone

and sewage from the hall floor, and holding his nose against the stench.

'Interesting question, James,' he said, letting go of his nose for a second. 'There is a theory that suggests that a thick concrete outer membrane, wrapped in a thin lead deflector or absorption shield, could . . . *Whooooaaahh!*'

Halfway through his theory, Alexander found himself dangling upside-down by his ankles, his head inches above the sewage-filled mop bucket.

'Oi! Get off! Whassup? Aaaargh!' Alexander cried, trying to wriggle clear of the stinking water. Gordon Carver just tightened his grip.

'Oi! Stick!' he grunted, giving Alexander a shake. A calculator and a laminated periodic table flew out of his blazer pocket. 'Was it you who showered us in maggots earlier?'

Alexander wriggled and writhed in vain. 'Who? Me? Would I do a thing like that? No, it was a bunch of ghosts!'

67

Lenny and James looked at each other.

'He doesn't do himself any favours, does he?' said Lenny.

'Are you making fun of me, Stick?' bellowed Gordon, lowering Alexander even closer to the rancid sewage.

'N-n-not at all!' cried Alexander, trying to keep his hair from touching the slime.

'If there's one thing I *hate*, apart from *you* of course, it's worms, slugs and slimy things!' shouted Gordon, shaking Alexander's ankles furiously. 'And a good dunking in this gunk should help you remember that!'

'No! Gordon! It wasn't me! Stop!' wailed Alexander, struggling frantically.

'I'm going to enjoy this!' grunted Gordon, lowering the headmaster's son another few centimetres.

Suddenly, Lenny had a brainwave. 'Doesn't like maggots, eh?' he muttered, grabbing a big juicy handful from his bin bag. 'We'll see about that!'

With one leap he bounded across the hall floor, kicked the sewage bucket out of the way and thrust the writhing handful of worms right down Gordon Carver's trousers.

The bully stood frozen with rage for a moment,

before dropping Alexander and frantically grappling with his trousers, slapping at his legs and rolling around on the floor.

'Get 'em off me!' he roared. 'I'll kill you for this! Get. Them. Off. Me. *Now!*'

'Run!' cried Lenny, helping Alexander to his feet.

The three boys charged out of the hall and down the corridor as fast as they could, leaving the bully to rid himself of the maggots on his own.

'Cheers, Lenny!' called Alexander over his shoulder as they ran. 'But what about a plan for tonight?'

'We'll just have to think something up this evening!' cried James as they burst out of the school door, and careered straight into Mr Tick.

'Oooof!' said the headmaster, untangling himself and straightening his tie. 'And what is the meaning of *this*?'

The boys stopped and caught their breath.

'We-we-we were just going to get some, erm . . . urgent props for the play tonight, dad!' said Alexander.

'Alexander! You know the rule!' frowned Mr Tick. 'Between the hours of nine o'clock in the morning and three-twenty in the afternoon, I'm your headmaster, not your dad!'

'Sorry, da– er, sir!' Alexander mumbled, blushing.

'Still, it's good to see you boys working hard on the play,' said Mr Tick. 'As you know, it's *very* important that Lord Goldsworthy is impressed. The school *badly needs* the new luxury offi– I mean, the *improvements* he's going to pay for!'

As the headmaster strode down the corridor, his mobile phone rang.

'Hello! Is that Barry's Jacuzzis? Yes, thank you for calling me back. I'm looking for something *big!*' the boys heard him say as he disappeared from view. 'The largest hot tub you sell – *money no object!*'

CHAPTER 8
FRIGHT NIGHT

'Looking *gooood*!' said Mr Tick to his reflection, adjusting his playing-cards tie. He reached over to his desk and picked up a comb and a ruler.

'Sideburns – six centimetres!' he said to himself, measuring them precisely. 'Hair – forty-five degrees exactly!' he muttered, combing it with the help of a protractor.

Finally, he bent down and polished his brand-new, mirror-shiny shoes with a special soft leather cloth. He admired his teeth in a gleaming toe.

'Looking great, Richard Tick!' he beamed.

'Ready for action!'

He was about to give himself a kiss in the mirror when Miss Keys burst into the room.

'Ooooh!' she said admiringly. 'You look *so* smart, Mr Tick!'

Mr Tick smiled. 'Why thank you, Miss Keys. I have made an extra effort today. Now, I just need to iron my shoelaces . . .'

'Actually, sir,' Miss Keys interrupted, 'I think you should go out to the school gate. Lord Goldsworthy is due any minute!'

Mr Tick gave his hair one last measure with the protractor and set off. 'Wish me luck, Miss Keys!' he called over his shoulder. 'We could have the money by this time tomorrow!'

He strode down the corridor, pausing to stick a pupil's painting over a big patch of mould on the wall on the way.

'Must see the school at its best,' he muttered to himself as he reached the school gate. 'Now – be nice to this lord, and that new office will be yours in no time!'

As he was waiting, he cast his eye over at the school sign. It was nailed to a dead tree, and the words 'St Sebastian's School' were totally obscured by bird poo and green mould. Some ancient ex-pupil had scribbled 'Keep out – haunted!' underneath it in dripping red paint.

'Does no one care about this school?' muttered Mr Tick. 'Mr Wharpley!' he yelled at the top of his voice. 'Get here, *now*!'

Reg Wharpley shuffled up to the front gate immediately. 'What is it now, Mr Tick? Only I've been told to hose down the swimming pool block after the er... *accident* last week!'

Mr Tick tutted. 'Never mind about that – this is *important*! Lord Goldsworthy is about to arrive, and that sign is a disgrace. Clean it up at once!'

Mr Wharpley sighed, fetched a paintbrush and some paint, and got to work.

He'd just finished the first 'S' when a huge
limousine roared round the corner, through the
school gate, and screeched to a halt inches from
Mr Tick. As it stopped, it splashed a huge spray of
mud and water all over the headmaster's smart suit
and shiny shoes.

'What the. . .?' cried Mr Tick, before calming
himself. 'Remember, *be nice!*' he muttered, and

75

opened the limo door. A tall old man with a huge diamond encrusted watch stepped out of the car.

'Why, Lord Goldsworthy, sir, m'Lord!' simpered Mr Tick. 'So good to . . . er . . .'

Lord Goldsworthy looked at Mr Tick's outstretched hand, and hung his briefcase on it, before he spotted Mr Wharpley.

'Reg, my old boy!' cried Lord Goldsworthy. 'How marvellous to see you!'

The caretaker smiled and hurried over.

'Why, I remember you as a young rascal round these parts!' said Reg, beaming at Lord Goldsworthy.

'And I remember you as a young caretaker!' smiled the Lord. 'Those were the days, weren't they, eh? The fun we used to get up to!'

'Ah, yes!' smiled Reg. 'And you must remember Mr Cross, the headmaster!'

Lord Goldsworthy seemed lost in a dream. 'Mr Cross! Why, of course! He was the best

headmaster ever!' he sighed.

'Ahem . . .' Mr Tick coughed politely.

'And he knew how to dress smartly, too!'
continued the Lord, frowning at Mr Tick's muddy
trousers and shoes.

'Ah! Yes, quite. How good of you to point that out, Lord Goldsworthy, sir!' Mr Tick smiled awkwardly. 'Now, if you'd like to come inside?'

Lord Goldsworthy gave Mr Wharpley's hand one final friendly squeeze and followed the headmaster.

'School's looking a bit tatty, Mr Tick!' he tutted.

'Well – yes. And the *headmaster's office* is rather run down, too!' said Mr Tick, showing Lord Goldsworthy to his seat. 'In fact, after the play, I have some plans for a new headmaster's block – perhaps you'd like to look them over?'

Lord Goldsworthy snorted as he sat down. 'New headmaster's office? Sounds expensive!' he said. 'Let's see what this play's like first!'

Mr Tick smiled through gritted teeth. 'Of course! Good idea! Now if you'll just excuse me, I have to wish the cast good luck!'

As he strode towards the backstage area, Mr Tick's false smile was replaced by a frown. He burst through the dressing-room door, sending Alexander flying into a heap in the corner.

'Get up, Alexander!' he shouted. 'This is no time for tomfoolery!'

The headmaster paced before the frightened cast. 'I'm going to say this very clearly, so you all understand!' he scowled. 'This play has to be good. It has to be *perfect*! And any pupil who forgets his lines, or is less than *amazing* will be facing *detentions* until they're drawing their pension!'

The cast groaned. 'And, Mr Thomas!' continued Mr Tick at the top of his voice. 'If I don't get my new luxury headmaster's offi– I mean, donation to the school – I will hold you *personally* responsible!'

As he turned and slammed the door, Lenny sighed. 'Somehow, I think forgetting our lines will be the least of our worries!' he said.

As he spoke, the first of the skeletons began filing into the room, their bones rattling loudly.

This was going to be a long night.

Down in the plague pit, Edith was standing on her barrel, punching her hand into her fist. In front of her, hundreds of skeletons were lined up, along with a few ghosts.

'This play has to be *awful*!' screamed Edith at the top of her hideous voice. 'It has to be *dreadful*! It has to be the *worst play ever*! And any skeleton or ghost who is less than *terrifying* will find the rest of their life a *total misery*!'

'But we're dead!' mumbled Ambrose.

'Oh, your *deaths* then!' screeched the disgusting old hag. 'This is no time for arguing! Now get up there and *cause some chaos*!'

The skeletons began to slowly file away.

'I suppose we might as well get this over with!' grumbled Ambrose to the Headless Horseman. 'We won't get a moment's peace until it's done . . .'

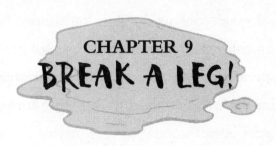

CHAPTER 9
BREAK A LEG!

James stood in the middle of the stage and looked at the crowd. The hall was packed with parents, with Lord Goldsworthy and Mr Tick in prime positions on the front row.

'Erm. . .' he began. He could already see some of the skeletons rattling their ribs in the wings.

'Get on with it!' hissed Mr Thomas.

James gulped and uttered his first line. 'W-we begin our story in a land ruled by a terrible skeleton army!' he began. Three skeletons lurched uncontrollably into the audience's view.

'Uh-oh!' mumbled James. 'Here we go!'

He tried to get his second line out, but more and more skeletons were piling on stage. They started crashing into each other and falling over, their bones tangling together and clattering to the floor with each collision. Big leg bones and tiny finger bones started to ping across the stage, banging off other skeletons and smacking into the actors.

'Oh! Here comes my fair love! The beautiful Ghouliet!' shouted James, trying to ignore the increasing chaos.

Stacey shuffled on stage, but two skeletons crashed into each other and their skulls flew off into the air, landing with a crunch at her feet.

'Ewwwww! Gross!' she cried, forgetting her first line. 'Slimy!'

A thick, gooey slime had begun to dribble out of the lighting rig and on to the stage floor. And each time a skeleton lost a limb, horrible black

sewage oozed out of its bone sockets and mingled with the slime, making a deadly, hissing mix that steamed with an eye-watering stench.

'Ahoy there! Is that Romeo?' bellowed Gordon Carver, limping on to the stage nursing a bruised arm. Behind him, the headless knight from the rehearsal was carrying the massive bloody sword *and* his own head under his arm.

'Er . . . Juliet!' shouted James, reeling from the hideous smell of the slime. 'My love for you makes me want to *sing a song*!'

As the orchestra tuned up, James surveyed the room. The audience was looking puzzled and a little scared. Lord Goldsworthy was rubbing his eyes and blinking. When he opened them again, the knight's severed head was balanced just opposite him on the front of the stage. It blew the Lord a long raspberry.

'Lordy-pants! Lordy-pants!' it mocked, before rolling off. Its body was racing round the stage, swinging its sword about and gleefully drop-kicking skulls into the crowd like footballs.

James slid over to Lenny. 'Do something!' he hissed. 'This is out of control!'

Lenny, however, was grappling with a skeleton.

'Get off!' he cried, bashing at the skeleton with a severed leg bone.

'It's probably just trying to be friendly!' said

James, pitching in with a sharp rib. 'Maybe it's a girl skeleton and it fancies you!'

Lenny finally booted it in the skull, sending it flying and causing the headless body to jolt off the edge of the stage, toppling into the orchestra pit.

'Yeah? Well it's better looking than the weird girl in year nine who fancies you!' Lenny replied, wiping some sewage off his tight black pyjamas.

Before James could answer back, the orchestra kicked in. But the horrible, creepy xylophone noise drowned them all out. He looked over, covering his ears. There was a ghostly man flickering in and out of view, bashing the rib cage of the skeleton Lenny had chucked into the pit like a xylophone.

'Aaaargh! Make it stop!'

'It's hideous!'

'Even worse than the orchestra!'

The ghost nodded in time with his ghastly melody, while the orchestra stared on in horror, backing away from the flickering being and the skeleton. A chill swept over the room, and the parents covered their ears against the morbid, horrible music.

CRASH!

TINKLE!

All round the room, windows, cups and glasses began to shatter as the ghostly music reached an even higher pitch. Mr Thomas wrapped his glasses in his jumper to protect them.

'Eeeeeeeeek! Aaaaaargh!'

One of the violinists in the orchestra screamed hysterically as she noticed her violin bow had been replaced by a rotting arm bone. She flung it across the orchestra, smacking Bertram in the face and putting a stop to the dreadful music at last.

'Phew!' sighed Alexander. 'That din was worse

than Dad singing in the shower!'

James took his hands away from his ears and stumbled forwards in a daze. Mr Tick was frowning and shaking his head.

'Er . . . Ghouliet! Your eyes are like . . . oh, forget it!' cried James, giving up on his lines as a grinning skeleton swung across the stage on the curtains. Ducking out of its way, James slithered along the slippery floor, and showered the front row in big dollops of sewage and greasy slime.

'Eugh!'

'Disgusting!'

'Argh! It burns!'

Mr Tick looked on in horror as a massive dollop landed right in Lord Goldsworthy's lap.

'Oh! So sorry! Allow me!' cried the headmaster, pulling out his hanky and dabbing furiously at the Lord's trousers. 'Must apologise! New . . . erm . . . special effects!' he mumbled.

'Get off me, you buffoon!' hissed Lord

Goldsworthy. The headmaster was distraught.

'You're right!' cried Mr Tick, leaping to his feet. 'I can't clean it off. Here! Have my trousers instead! I insist!'

And with that, the headmaster whipped off his trousers and thrust them in Lord Goldsworthy's face. Some parents gasped at the sight of Mr Tick's bright green 'Solitaire Champ' boxer shorts – but Miss Keys stood up with her camera and tried to take a sneaky photo.

While Lord Goldsworthy was struggling to breathe through Mr Tick's trousers, a greasy skull catapulted off the stage and smacked the headmaster in the head with a crunch. He went flying back, landing with a thump in his seat. Lord Goldsworthy looked relieved.

'The curtain! Drop the curtain! Early interval!' screamed James, staring aghast at the trouserless headmaster and slime-covered Lord. He leapt aside as three skeletons skidded on their faces

across the slime, crashing in a splintering shower
of broken bones in front of Gordon Carver.

'I said drop the curtain! *Now!*' roared James. As
the curtain fell and blocked the stage from view,
he dragged a struggling, armless skeleton behind
it by the big toe.

The room went quiet. The audience was frozen
with their mouths open. Mr Tick sheepishly put

his trousers back on. Lord Goldsworthy said nothing.

After a minute, the headmaster broke the silence.

'So . . .' he said, buckling up his belt. 'Anyone for an ice cream?'

At the back of the hall, a disgusting old crone in a dinner lady's outfit rubbed her hands together and squeezed her frizzy, wiry hair into a blonde wig from the costumes' cupboard.

'It's all going to plan!' cackled Edith. 'The Lord is horrified! They'll *never* get their new block now! Ha, ha, ha, haaaaaa!'

CHAPTER 10
I SCREAM

'Out the way! Let me through!'

James stumbled off stage and headed for the dressing room. He kicked open the door, but it only budged a few centimetres.

'Oi! Open up! It's me!' he shouted, and leant harder on the door. When he got his head round it, he saw the problem – *skeletons*. Loads of skeletons, all crammed into the dressing room. Some of them were playing jacks in a corner. Others were chewing on maggots. One was smearing make-up on his skull in the mirror.

The actual cast of the play was lined up against the wall outside, looking terrified.

'Oh, I give up!' James groaned, and sloped off to find his friends. 'Those skeletons are driving me crazy!'

He passed Mr Thomas in the corridor. The drama teacher was pacing up and down, wringing his beret in his hands.

'I'll get the sack!' he whimpered. 'I'll never make it to Hollywood! I'm doomed!'

James ignored him and eventually found his friends hiding behind some old scenery. He sat down next to Alexander and helped himself to a jelly baby from Lenny's pocket.

'Well, Mr Thomas doesn't seem too cheery!' he said. 'He's worried he'll never make it to Hollywood!'

'That's one thing we *can't* blame the ghosts for!' Lenny scoffed. 'The play was awful *before* they got involved!'

'Yes. It looks like it's *curtains* for Mr Thomas!' joked Alexander, scanning his friends' faces for any hint of laughter.

Nothing.

'I wouldn't laugh at that joke if I'd just inhaled laughing gas. Let alone when we're in mortal danger from a bunch of crazed spooks!' said Lenny with a scowl.

'Too right!' said James. 'This is no time for joking around! What are we gonna do to stop this carnage?'

Lenny looked thoughtful. 'What do we know about these ghosts, then?' he asked. 'What are their weaknesses?'

James thought for a moment. 'We know they're slimy, already dead, and can disappear when they want,' he said. 'That doesn't strike me as particularly weak.'

'We know their favourite food, though!' said Alexander.

'Really?' said James. 'What is it?'

'*I scream!* Geddit?' cried Alexander, collapsing into fits of laughter.

Lenny and James looked at him, unamused.

'We could feed them Alexander and do a runner?' said Lenny, hopefully.

'Nah. They'd never have him!' replied James.

'Oi!' said Alexander.

'Well, in case you hadn't noticed, things are rather unpleasant on that stage, Stick!' cried James. 'It's all right for you – you're at the back with the spotlight!'

'Oh, I'm just trying to *lighten* the mood here!' said Alexander. 'I've memorised all the theatre jokes from my humour database and . . . mmphmph! *Mumphumphmmmpff!*'

He scowled and spat out the jester's hat James had grabbed from a costumes' box and stuffed in his mouth.

'Oh, stop arguing and start thinking!' cried Lenny, jumping up. 'Someone is going to get hurt out there! Stacey's already got a sprained wrist from where a skeleton bundled her over!'

James stood up too, and started pacing up and down. 'Right then. Let's think of a plan. And save the rubbish jokes for later, Alexander!'

'Yeah. *Much* later!' added Lenny.

Alexander frowned and started thinking hard.

William sat invisibly watching his would-be friends, wishing he could materialise and join in. It had been over 600 years since he'd had a friend his own age, and he desperately want to be part of their gang. But he doubted whether they'd appreciate a dead eleven-year-old as a mate.

Suddenly, his ears pricked up at something Lenny said.

'Stacey? Injured?' whispered William. 'Not *Stacey*! This has gone *too far*!'

He jumped off his chair and floated through the wall, leaving the three friends to think up a plan. He found Ambrose lurking in the corridor outside the dressing room.

'Hey, Ambrose!' cried William, still invisible. 'Have you seen Edith anywhere? It's time we put a stop to this!'

Ambrose shrugged. 'She's out front, I think,' he replied.

William didn't stop to chat. He drifted right through the stage wall and out into the hall, scanning the crowd of parents for any sign of the haggard old crone. He didn't have to search long.

At the back of the room, holding an ice-cream tray, was a very badly disguised Edith. She had a dinner lady's apron wrapped round her filthy rags, and a ridiculous blonde wig squeezed over her rotting frizzy hair.

'Ice cream! Get your ice creams here!' she croaked. A few parents lined up in front of her.

'Groargh! I think I'm going to . . .'

One of the dads ran from the hall clutching his mouth.

'Aaaargh! This stuff is . . . bleurgh!'

A mum dashed for the toilets, hurling her ice cream in the bin as she ran. William drifted over and inspected Edith's ice-cream tray. As he

expected, it wasn't ice cream she was dishing up.

'Groooeurgh!' cried another dad, clutching his stomach. 'That's the grossest thing I've ever eaten!'

'And you used to have the school dinners here, dear!' said his wife, shocked.

Inside the pots marked 'chocolate', thick sewer slime gave off a rancid stench. In the 'vanilla' pots, maggots writhed around in a putrid white goo.

'Er . . . Edith? Can I have a word?' whispered William in her ear.

But Edith didn't even notice. She was busy dishing up more of her disgusting tubs to the ice-cream queue, a big, foul grin plastered across her flaky face.

'Oh, she'll never back down now!' sighed William, drifting backstage again. 'If I'm going to put a stop to this, I'll have to do it myself!'

He found his three friends still plotting to foil the ghosts in the second half of the play.

Don't worry! he thought to himself. *I'll be helping you out!*

And with that, he drifted off to find Stacey. That sprained wrist could be nasty, after all . . .

'I'm *so* sorry, Lord Goldsworthy, sir!' grovelled Mr Tick. 'I don't know *what* happened during the first half! I'll have very stern words with our drama teacher! Please stay!'

Lord Goldsworthy sighed. 'Oh, very well! And less of your snivelling!'

Mr Tick sat down again and smoothed his tie. 'Oh, thank you, Lord Goldsworthy, sir!' he simpered. 'Now – about this new headmaster's office!' he began. 'Initial costs suggest that we could get a very ... erm ... *modest* one built for around ...'

'I told you, Tick, I'm not talking about my donation until after the play!' interrupted Lord Goldsworthy, eyeing his ice cream suspiciously.

'Yes, yes. Of course! After the play, sir!' said Mr Tick, tucking an architect's plan back into his jacket pocket.

As the curtain rose for the second half, Mr Tick scowled at the stage. He would *not* let a bunch of idiotic pupils ruin the office of his dreams!

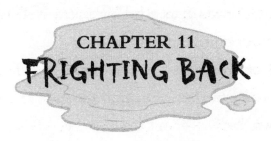

CHAPTER 11
FRIGHTING BACK

A scared hush fell over the audience as the curtain jerked upwards. A horrified gasp went up at what it revealed: a scene of *total carnage* that wouldn't have been out of place in a horror film.

The stage was rammed with skeletons, all doing skids in the slime. The Headless Horseman was booting his head around like a football, closely followed by Ambrose, who kept trying to tackle him with his decomposing right foot. Bertram was sitting in the orchestra, bashing away at another set of skeleton's ribs, his eyes glowing red and ectoplasm dribbling out of his nose.

'Attack!' cried James, lunging at a skeleton with a wooden prop sword. 'Take that!'

The skeleton grabbed a leg bone to defend himself and started whacking James round the head with it.

'Aaaaargh! Help!' wailed James.

Lenny pitched in, but was sent flying by one of Ambrose's sliding tackles. He landed with a splat in a pool of slime, showering goo over a quivering Stacey.

'Ewwwwww!' she screamed. 'Make this *stop*!'

William, watching from the wings, sprang into action. Drifting across the hall, he floated over to Alexander, who was watching helplessly from the back of the room, slumped over his spotlight.

'Whoah! What the . . .' cried Alexander, as his spotlight switched itself on underneath him, and started swivelling about. 'Whoah there!'

William narrowed his eyes and aimed the spotlight straight at a skeleton on the stage. He flicked it on to 'full beam'.

After a second, the skeleton exploded in a shower of splintered bone and sewage, letting out a terrible scream as it went.

'Aha! I get it!' cried Alexander, wrestling control of the spotlight back from his invisible

helper. 'They're allergic to bright light! An interesting phenomenon!'

He swung the beam to and fro across the stage, picking off the skeletons one by one like they were baddies in a computer game.

'Take that!' he cried, whooping at each one that blew up. 'Alexander to the rescue!'

Lord Goldsworthy jumped as another skeleton exploded in a shower of goo on the stage. 'Wh-wh–' he whimpered.

'Ah, yes. We're very proud of our, erm . . . *special effects* department here at St Sebastian's!' Mr Tick shouted over the skeletons' screams.

James covered his face to protect it from a shower of flying bone and sewage, and ducked to the front of the stage. He had an idea.

Snapping his braces off his shoulders, he grabbed a Roman spear from a terrified cast member and wrapped his braces round the end of it, making a makeshift catapult.

'Come here, you!' he cried, seizing the horseman's head as it rolled past his feet. 'It's cannon-ball time!'

He wrapped the head in his braces, propped the spear on his knee and pulled back as hard as he could.

'Nnnnng!' he strained, giving the catapult one last tug. 'Three-two-one . . . *Fire!*'

The horseman's head rocketed right over the audience and crashed through the one remaining unbroken window.

'Ah, yes. We've got a very good, erm ... *stunt man* training programme here at St Sebastian's!' said Mr Tick, as Lord Goldsworthy looked on aghast.

The horseman's body sprang into action, leapt off the stage and charged out of the window after its head. James could see it chasing across the school field after the bouncing bonce.

'Yesss! It worked!' cried James, ducking another shower of skeleton remains.

'Nice one, mate!' cried Lenny, tripping up a passing skeleton. 'I knew those braces would come in handy!'

'Yeah! Now we just need to find a use for your skin-tight PJs!' laughed James.

William, meanwhile, was still at work. He sidled up alongside Ambrose, who was tearing round the stage whooping and swivelling his eyeballs at the audience. Keeping himself invisible, he reached into Ambrose's pocket and pulled a big handful of wriggling leeches out.

'Eh? What are these?' cried Lenny, feeling a squelchy, wriggly lump pressed into his right hand. 'Where did they come from?' He watched the leeches slithering about and had a brainwave.

'The Gorilla!' he exclaimed, and dodged out the way of Ambrose, who was foaming at the mouth for extra effect.

'Gordon! Over here!' cried Lenny. Gordon was enjoying himself, bashing skeletons and cast members alternately with a big thigh bone. He stopped as Lenny approached.

'I thought you might like *these*!' cried Lenny, and stuffed the leeches down the bully's trousers. 'I know you love slimy things!'

The bully turned bright red and raised his huge fist to bash Lenny. But before he could swing the punch, the leeches started to bite.

'Why you little . . . *Aaaaaaaaaaaaargh*! They're biting!' wailed Gordon. 'Owwww! Ow! Ow! Ow! Ow! *Ow*!'

Hopping from one foot to the other, he dived off the stage, stuffing both hands down his trousers and doing a frenzied jig as he tried to scoop the leeches off his skin.

'Get them off me!' he wailed, crashing into the audience, out the other side, and through the hall door at the back of the room, his legs flying around like a tap-dancer on fast-forward.

'Is that boy all right?' asked a shocked Lord Goldsworthy.

'Aha! Yes!' Mr Tick replied, scratching his head. 'He's one of our best . . . erm . . . *dance* students!'

William, meanwhile, was watching Ambrose.

'Any . . . minute . . . *now*!' he said.

Ambrose stopped foaming, reached into his pocket, and frowned.

'My leeches! Where are my leeches?' he cried.
Lenny pointed silently at the rapidly
disappearing Gordon.

'Why, the great big thief!' Ambrose muttered,
leaping off the stage. 'Gimme my leeches back!'

Lenny watched the ghost charge out of the
hall after Gordon, dragging Bertram after him.
'Help me get my leeches back!' Lenny heard him
cry as the ghosts disappeared out the door.

'Good one, Lenny!' cried James, giving his
friend a high-five. 'We've nearly got 'em all!'

'Yeah! We should turn professional!' said
Lenny. 'Now how about we perform a line or
two?'

James bounded to the front of the stage, where
Stacey was curled in a terrified ball by the
curtains.

'Oh, Ghouliet, if only we could be together,
but your evil father would never allow it!' he
cried.

Stacey looked up at James like he was insane. She let forth a little whimper.

James looked out at the audience. People were ducking under their programmes and covering their eyes and ears. Lord Goldsworthy's jaw was hanging open in shock, his eyes fixed on the stage, shards of bone sticking out of his hair.

'Well, I must say!' said Mr Tick nervously. 'We're . . . erm . . . very proud of our . . .'

But the headmaster couldn't think of *anything* to explain the horror they had just witnessed.

CHAPTER 12
ODD'S WALLOP

'You imbeciles! Get back here *now*!' screeched Edith, ripping off her wig. 'That's not in the plan!'

As the Headless Horseman, Bertram and Ambrose all disappeared from view, Edith rolled up the rags on her scrawny arms.

'Fine!' she muttered. 'If you want a play haunting properly, *do it yourself*!'

Striding across the hall, she tore off her apron, raised her arms in the air and jumped on to the stage with a blood-curdling scream.

'Aaaaaaargh!' she howled, whirling round to

face the audience. 'St Sebastian's – *I'm going to kill you all*!'

Lenny and James froze mid high-five.

'W-w-what is *that*?' stuttered Lenny.

James shuddered. 'Dunno!' he said. 'But it's uglier than your school photo!'

Edith was looking even more disgusting than usual. Her wiry ginger hair was standing on end, and clumps of it were dropping out as she ranted and raved. Ectoplasm and bits of rotten tooth were flying from her gnashing jaws, and her eyes were bulging to twice their normal size and swivelling about madly.

'You like plays, do you?' the old crone screeched at the horrified audience in a voice like scraping metal. 'Then play with *this*!'

James and Lenny watched on, horrified, as Edith hitched up her skirts and started kicking great splashes of slime and sewage over the crowd.

The headmaster dived in front of Lord

Goldsworthy, but it was no use. The Lord spat and retched as a dollop of goo flew right into his open mouth.

'Feel free to stop her when you feel like it!' said Lenny.

'Can I wait until she hits Mr Tick first?' asked James.

But Edith was just getting going. With a hideous

cackle, she started to spin round and round on the stage, stamping her knobbly feet and whirling her arms about. She span faster and faster until there was a mini whirlwind in the hall.

'*This is it*, St Sebastian's!' she howled as she span.

Bones, wooden swords and broken skulls started to fly into the air and spin around Edith. The audience's chairs started rattling and shuffling towards the awful tornado.

'We've got to do something!' cried Lenny.

'*I'll kill you alllll!*' cried her blood-curdling voice from the centre of the storm. The audience was scrabbling around holding on to their seats as Edith's whirlwind threatened to suck them in.

William shielded his eyes and sprang into action. He leapt on to the stage and grabbed Lenny and James by the hands, dragging them backstage and into the dressing room.

'Eh?' cried Lenny, as something invisible pulled him along the corridor. 'What *now*?'

William stopped in front of the dressing-room mirror, picked up an eyeliner pencil and began to write.

Lenny and James watched in amazement as a message appeared letter by letter in front of them.

'Remember!' it read, as the pencil seemed to write the words unaided. 'She hates the plague!'

'Eh? What's that got to do with anything?' cried Lenny. 'We haven't got time for cryptic clues!'

But James was frantically scrabbling through the make-up box, chucking tubes and brushes over his shoulder.

'James! I know you like to look your best, but this is no time for a makeover!' said Lenny, ducking a flying mascara.

'Got it!' cried James, holding a stick of red lipstick in his right hand. 'Lenny! Come here!'

Lenny groaned. 'James, I've had enough lipstick smeared on me over the years by my big sis and Stacey. I don't need you doing it, too!'

James grabbed Lenny by the neck and started drawing big boils and buboes on his face with the lipstick.

'Lenny – you're going to regret telling me that for the rest of your life. But we've got a job to do first!'

Lenny looked at his reflection as James started drawing buboes on his own face and arms.

'I get it! The plague!' cried Lenny. 'We're scaring her off!'

'Three cheers for the brain of Britain!' said James, his face covered in spots. 'Let's go get her!'

The two boys charged down the corridor and back on to the stage, where Edith was raining a fierce shower of bone, splintered wood and gobs of slime on the audience with an evil grin plastered over her face.

'Oi! Ugly!' cried James.

'Over here!' shouted Lenny, pretending to cough and stagger.

Edith stopped and turned to the boys, her grin fading instantly. All the levitating skulls and bones dropped to the floor with a clatter.

'Boils? Staggering? They've got the p–p–plague!' she hissed. 'Get away from me! Get back!'

James and Lenny started to lurch towards Edith, clutching their stomachs and groaning.

'Ohhh, these buboes are awful!' James droned in a weak voice.

'Bleurgh!' Lenny coughed, clutching his sides. 'I don't feel too good!'

Edith started to back away across the stage. 'Get away! I'm not catching that wretched disease twice!' she shrieked. 'It's already killed me once!'

'Ohhhhhh,' wailed James, walking like a zombie towards the old hag. 'I think I need a hug!'

Edith backed off even further.

'Don't touch me!' she cried.

'Oargh!' Lenny groaned. 'Me too! I need a . . . whoah!'

As he staggered towards Edith, he tripped on a skull and flew through the air at her. Edith screamed and leapt off the stage.

'I said get away from me!' she howled. 'Get away from meeeeeeeee!'

As Lenny picked himself up, the rotten old crone turned on her heels and fled, crashing through the doors at the back of the hall and vanishing into

the night with a disgusting, grating scream.

James and Lenny wiped their faces and turned to the crowd. Alexander was still wielding his spotlight, and turned it on the last three skeletons left on stage. They blew up immediately, drenching the horrified audience in more shattered bone and sewer slime. Lord Goldsworthy winced as a broken skull smashed him on the head, covering his hair with specks of rotting brain.

'Eugh!'

'Aaaaargh!'

SPLAT!

As the dust settled and the final drops of slime rained down on Mr Tick's sodden hair, James and Lenny surveyed the scene.

'This doesn't look good!' mumbled James.

The first four rows were absolutely drenched in sewage. The whole audience had slime and splinters of bone stuck to their faces and hair, and some of them were still retching and heaving thanks to Edith's ice creams. Most of the mums were silently shaking and crying, and several of the dads were cowering under their seats, frantically babbling into their mobile phones for help.

'I think they noticed the ghosts!' said Lenny, picking a bone out of his nose.

Worst of all, in the front row, Lord Goldsworthy was curled in a ball on his chair, rocking backwards and forwards, a strange whimpering noise coming out of his nose. He was drenched in slime and sewage, and had a skeleton's tooth stuck in his well-groomed hair.

Next to him, Mr Tick was shaking with a mixture of rage and terror, his hands clenched into tight fists. The grinding of his teeth was the only noise in the hushed, petrified room.

'Tough crowd!' said James. 'Let's see if they like the final scene!'

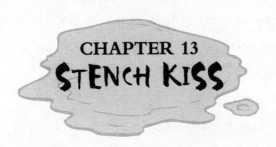

CHAPTER 13
STENCH KISS

James helped a bewildered Stacey to her feet and dragged her to the front of the stage. The silent audience barely seemed to notice.

'And so concludes our tale of woe!' said James, trying to rally Stacey into saying her lines.

'Er . . . farewell, my lovely Romeo!' Stacey stuttered, remembering how the play ended. She shut her eyes and leant in to give James a kiss on the cheek.

'Mwah!'

'Ewwwww!'

Some confused parents thought they saw a
ghostly head appear out of thin air and intercept
Stacey's kiss. But they were so bewildered by now
that they hardly even noticed.

'You're ice-cold, James!' whispered Stacey. 'And a
bit slimy, too!'

She rubbed her lips and grimaced. Behind
James, an invisible William snuck away, rubbing

his cheek. He couldn't help it — he just *had* to steal that kiss from Stacey!

The audience barely moved as the curtain dropped. There was no applause. Some parents at the back began to creep cautiously towards the door, sprinting for their cars as soon as they got outside.

'Ohhhhhh!' Mr Tick groaned, holding his head in his hands. 'I'm *so* sorry, Lord Goldsworthy!' He pulled the luxury office plan out of his pocket, screwed it up and threw it on the floor. 'I won't be needing *that* any more!' he sighed, and looked over at the Lord next to him.

To his absolute amazement, Lord Goldsworthy was sitting up in his chair, beaming from ear to ear. Mr Tick rubbed his eyes in disbelief. That whimpering — it couldn't have been *laughter,* could it?

'Ha, ha, ha, ha, ha! Marvellous!' cried the Lord, clapping loudly. None of the parents joined in.

'Marvellous! Absolutely marvellous!' Lord Goldsworthy chuckled, wiping the slime from his face. 'Best play I've seen in years!'

Mr Tick's jaw dropped. 'You mean you *liked* it?' the headmaster asked, astounded.

'Liked it? I *loved* it!' cried Lord Goldsworthy. 'Such amazing special effects! Such audience participation! So challenging! So funny! How

124

could I not like it?'

Mr Tick grabbed his screwed-up architect's plan, and began carefully unfolding it.

'Yes, well, I'm certainly . . . erm . . . very proud of our drama department!' he smiled. 'And I personally oversaw the amazing – erm . . . *special effects*!'

Lord Goldsworthy stopped clapping and turned to Mr Tick. 'Well, all I can say is, I'd be glad to make my donation to the school!' he beamed.

'Yessss!' cried Mr Tick, punching the air, before pulling himself together and straightening his soggy tie.

'In that case, perhaps we should go over the plans for my new office!' he said, smoothing out the crumpled paper. He began explaining it to Lord Goldsworthy.

'You see,' he started, 'the wide-screen TV will go *here*, next to the jacuzzi. And the tropical fish tank will go . . .'

'Office? *Office?*' bellowed the Lord, interrupting Mr Tick. 'I'm not spending my money on an *office!*'

Mr Tick looked surprised. 'But it's what this school *really* needs!' he protested.

'Nonsense!' said Lord Goldsworthy. 'What this school needs is a fantastic new *drama studio* for this brilliant drama department of yours! *That's* what I'll spend my donation on!'

Mr Tick scrunched up the plan again, his shoulders drooping. 'A drama studio?' he moaned. 'But what about *me?*'

Lord Goldsworthy laughed. 'You must be very pleased, I know! After all, you did say how proud you were of your drama department!'

Mr Tick opened his mouth to protest, but the Lord interrupted him again. 'No no! Don't thank me! I'll send my best builders round to start work next week.' And with that, he wiped the goo out of his hair, jumped up and strode out of the hall.

Mr Tick slumped back down in his seat. Miss

Keys approached him timidly and began wiping some of the slime off his drenched hair with a towel.

'You look exhausted, Mr Tick!' she said, picking a toe bone out of his ear. 'Why don't you relax over a nice game of solitaire?'

Mr Tick squelched his toes in his ruined new shoes. 'You know what, Miss Keys?' he said. 'I think I will!'

James, Lenny and Alexander peered round the door of the dressing room. Mr Thomas was on the phone in the corridor, talking to a Hollywood agent.

'Yes, yes, I have lots of experience in the . . . erm . . . *horror* field!' he said, slipping his shades back on.

'Experience hiding in the costume cupboard that is!' said Lenny.

'I have an idea for a new film!' Mr Thomas continued. 'It's a film about zombie cowboys. Set in space. The main character . . . hello? . . . *hello?*'

Mr Thomas put the phone down and sighed.

'Doesn't look like we'll be seeing a Mr Thomas blockbuster any time soon!' said James, as the three boys started to peel off their slime-covered costumes.

'You won't be seeing me in a play any time soon, either!' grunted Lenny. 'That was one of the worst nights of my life!'

'Don't say that, Lenny!' cried James. 'Don't deprive the world of your tight black pyjamas and pasty white stomach!'

'Shut it, you!' said Lenny, giving James a shove. 'At least Stacey didn't say I had a cold, slimy face!'

'Hey, she never even kissed me!' said James. 'Anyway, I haven't forgotten about her and your sister and the make-up, remember!'

Lenny glared at him and dried the sludge off his

128

feet. 'I'll tell you one thing I thought I'd never say,' he said. 'Stick – you were right. That *was* worse than science with Mr Watts!'

Alexander punched the air. 'Yesss! I knew you'd come round! Science *is* fun, isn't it?'

'Well, it's more fun than writhing around in sewage with a bunch of murderous ghosts!' said Lenny.

'Wow! That's the nicest thing you've ever said about it!' gulped Alexander. 'Now, what do you call a ghost with no arms?'

James let out a long groan.

'*Armless!*' guffawed Alexander.

Lenny dropped his head into his hands. 'And there was me thinking the pain was over!'

Down in the plague pit, a furious Edith was ranting at the assembled ghosts.

'That was abysmal! The worst performance I've ever seen! I'm ashamed to call you ghosts!' the old hag screeched, pausing only to catch her breath.

Ambrose, the Headless Horseman and Bertram were all stretched out on the floor, completely ignoring her.

'I'll tell you what, it's nice down here with those skeletons gone, isn't it?' said Bertram, putting his feet up. A huge dollop of sewage flew out of a pipe and splattered him in the face.

'I'm not sure I'd say *nice*, Bertram!' said Ambrose. 'It's better though, eh, William?'

But William was in a dream, rubbing his left cheek over and over again. He didn't care how angry Edith was, Stacey Carmichael had *kissed him*. And that was enough to keep him happy for at *least* another 650 years!

SURNAME: Thomas

FIRST NAME: Edwin

AGE: 42

HEIGHT: 1.8 metres

EYES: Brown

HAIR: Black, a bit greasy

LIKES: Watching black-and-white films; writing his own masterpieces and sending them to Hollywood agents (who normally don't ring back!); dreaming of directing the world's best actors on million-dollar movies

DISLIKES: Being stuck in a rotten old school, directing children in rubbish school plays

SPECIAL SKILL: Writing a school play on any subject, usually based on whatever's in the prop cupboard

INTERESTING FACT: Mr Thomas is so confident he's about to be snapped up to work on a Hollywood movie, he keeps a bag packed by his bed so he can fly out any minute. It contains a copy of his latest play, some sunglasses and a bottle of fake tan but he has never needed it yet . . .

For more facts on Edwin Thomas, go to www.too-ghoul.com

Alexander Tick's
Joke File

(page 5,142)

Q What sleeps at the bottom of the sea?

A A kipper!

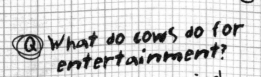

Q What do cows do for entertainment?

A They rent moovies!

Q Did you hear about the stupid tap dancer?

A He fell in the sink!

Q How do you make a bandstand?

A Take away their chairs!

NOTE TO SELF: input these into jokes database at earliest convenience

Q What do you call a snowman with a sun tan?

A A puddle!

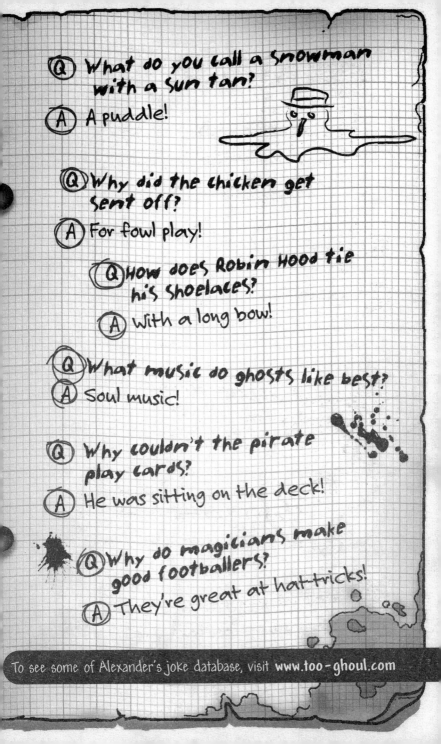

Q Why did the chicken get sent off?

A For fowl play!

Q How does Robin Hood tie his shoelaces?

A With a long bow!

Q What music do ghosts like best?

A Soul music!

Q Why couldn't the pirate play cards?

A He was sitting on the deck!

Q Why do magicians make good footballers?

A They're great at hat-tricks!

To see some of Alexander's joke database, visit www.too-ghoul.com

Bubonic Plagu

By make-up expert, Lenny Maxwell *

You will need:

A stick of lipstick
Some white powder
A mirror
A ghost to frighten

Step 1: Close the door and barricade it shut. For a proper makeover, you mustn't be disturbed by rampaging spooks. Sit in front of the mirror and open your make-up box

Step 2: Apply thick layer of white powder to your face, neck and arms. And any other bits of skin that are on show

Step 3: Use the lipstick to draw big red boils all over your face and arms. Add some oozing blood effects round your mouth, too

Nakeover Guide

Step 4: Ruffle your hair up and practise rolling your eyes in a zombie-like fashion

Step 5: Adopt a lurching, stiff walk and groan loudly as you move about the room

Step 6: Scare off any nearby ghosts. Or just give your mum a fright if there aren't any spooks around

*Top Tips:

Your big sister might not be amused when you've used all her lipstick on gruesome boils, so ask first!

Don't put the lipstick back in your pocket. It could be tricky to explain to your mates!

Ode to Stacey

By William Scroggins *

Stacey oh Stacey
You are so prettie
Your hair it is golden
And not at all nittie
Your mouth's full of teethe
And not rotting stumps
If my heart wasn't rotten
You'd make it go thump!
Your eyes don't go redde
And your blood isn't green
Which makes you the prettiest
Ladie I've seene!

* With help from Ambrose Harbottle,
who went to school once

Can't wait for the next book in the series?
Here's a sneak preview of

HIGH VOLTAGE!

available now from all good bookshops,
or **www.too-ghoul.com**

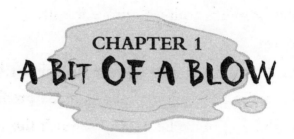

CHAPTER 1
A BIT OF A BLOW

For a moment, Lenny Maxwell thought his ears were going to blow clean off. The wind hadn't let up in days. In fact, it seemed to get stronger every morning, until the rain was flying sideways at such speed that you actually looked in the mirror whenever you got indoors just to check that you still had a face.

Yesterday, he, James and Alexander had spent lunch break leaning forwards into the blast with their arms stretched out to either side, seeing how far they could tip without actually falling over. Alexander had claimed to have reached an angle of 38 degrees, and had spent the first five minutes of maths trying to prove it with a protractor.

But that, of course, was when they didn't have anything else to get done. Today's lunch break wasn't shaping up to be nearly as much fun as yesterday's. In fact, it was shaping up to be one of the worst lunch hours in history. Lenny let the door bang back in his face, put down the pile of chairs he was carrying and tied his scarf tightly around his head. He didn't mind doing Mr Tick a favour, but he wasn't going to lose his ears for anyone.

He pushed the door open once again and stepped out into the playground. Alexander ran towards him, veering from side to side as buffets of wind pushed him around and very nearly sending Lenny and his pile of chairs flying.

'Oi!' shouted Lenny, just in time. Alexander

lurched to the left and screeched to a halt.

'Sorry,' he bellowed over the wind. 'Didn't see
you there. I'm going to get some more chairs.'

'Where's James?' hollered Lenny.

'Helping my father set up the table,' yelled
Alexander, and ran on through the door into the
school.

Lenny shrugged and stumbled on across playground. At least, he thought, I'm getting out of double geography. And I might even get a better report at parents' night for being helpful. Even storm clouds have silver linings. Can't wait for lunchtime, though. I'm so hungry I could eat one of Mrs Meadows's spinach casseroles.

Two steps later, he remembered the way the spinach slid down your throat if you didn't take time to chew it properly.

Well, maybe not that hungry, he thought.

In the playground, Mr Downe, the religious studies teacher, Mr Watts, the science teacher and the PE teacher, Ms Legg, stood with their hands on their hips and discussed the old tin shed the headmaster had installed there.

'He is joking, isn't he?' asked Mr Watts.

Mr Downe shook his head. 'Mr Tick,' he said,

'is known for many things, but his sense of humour is not one of them.'

'Yes, but,' said Mr Watts, 'this time he has to be joking. It looks like it's left over from the Second World War.'

'Or even the First World War,' said Ms Legg. 'It's bound to leak.'

'I think,' said Mr Watts, 'that's why he hired it in the first place, isn't it?'

The three sighed and rolled their eyes. St Sebastian's had not been weathering the storms well. After days of high winds, several tiles had been ripped clean off the roof, and the main hall's ceiling now had exactly one dozen constant dribbling leaks. Mr Wharpley, the caretaker, had filled the hall with buckets, but it was obvious that the forthcoming parents' evening could not take place there. So Mr Tick had hired the shed, and James, Alexander and Lenny had been chosen to help him prepare it.

Inside the hut, James Simpson was hauling a table from one side of the hut to another while the headmaster sat on a chair, 'Solitaire Champ' mug in hand, issuing orders to his secretary, Miss Keys.

'There won't be room to have everyone in here at once, of course,' he said. 'We'll have to have a holding area in the cloakrooms and send them over in groups.'

'Yes, headmaster,' said Miss Keys, scribbling frantically on her notepad.

'And I suppose we'd better lay on tea,' he said, 'while they wait. Tell Mrs Cooper, will you?'

'Yes, headmaster,' chirped Miss Keys, and scribbled some more.

'And Mr Wharpley had better make sure the toilets are gleaming,' he said. 'The last thing we need is complaints.'

'Yes, headmaster,' she squeaked again. So much to do!

The door scraped open, and the three teachers entered, followed by a dripping-wet Lenny.

'There you are, boy!' cried Mr Tick. 'Where on earth have you been?'

Lenny put down his pile of chairs and shook himself off like a shaggy dog. 'Fetching chairs like you asked me to, sir,' he said.

'Well, get on with it!' said Mr Tick. 'No time for slacking! James will get a hernia if he has to carry that table all by himself.'

The three teachers looked about them. The hut was as gloomy as their expressions, lit only by two naked light bulbs, the walls painted a dingy, dirty green. Their breath hung in the air like a cloud in front of them. Ms Legg shivered and pulled the collar of her tracksuit up to her ears.

'So, what do you think?' asked the headmaster.

It took a moment before anyone could think of anything to say. The walls echoed with the wind outside; it was like standing inside a biscuit tin while a toddler used it for a drum.

'It's a bit cold,' said Mr Downe.

'Beggars can't be choosers,' said Mr Tick, who was wearing three jumpers under his overcoat.

'Are you expecting us to sit in here all night without any heating? It's freezing!' said Mr Watts.

'Nothing a vest won't sort out,' said Mr Tick.

'But what about the parents? We can't expect them all to have turned up with vests on. They'll freeze to death!' said Ms Legg. 'Aren't there any heaters?'

Mr Tick looked reluctant. 'We can't just go turning heaters on because of a spot of rain,' he said.

The three teachers stood in silence and folded their arms.

'Oh, very well,' said Mr Tick.

He gestured towards a pair of ancient gas heaters that stood in the corner. They were painted a sludge brown and had patches of rust and scorch marks on the sides. 'Bought them second-hand yesterday,' he said. 'Still cost an arm and a leg.'

Another gust of wind shook the flimsy tin walls and a bolt of lightning split the sky. Mr Watts tucked his scarf firmly into his collar. The storm was taking a turn for the worse.